GIRLS ROCK!
Contents

CHAPTER 1
Cut Out for Netball?   1

CHAPTER 2
Ball Robbers   6

CHAPTER 3
Bulldog Boy and Snail Boy   13

CHAPTER 4
It's Not Over Yet   21

CHAPTER 5
Final Showdown   26

EXTRA STUFF

• Netball Lingo   33

• Netball Must-dos   34

• Netball Instant Info   36

• Think Tank   38

• Hey Girls! (Author Letter)   40

• When We Were Kids   42

• What a Laugh

Rachel

Ellie

CHAPTER 1

Cut Out for Netball?

Best friends Ellie and Rachel are
playing with Ellie's new netball at
their local netball court.

Rachel "This ball's so good. It feels
really nice. You must be thrilled
that your mum bought it for you."

Rachel aims for the netball ring
and shoots. It's a perfect shot. The
ball drops right through the ring and
falls to the ground.

Ellie "Yes, I suppose so. She thought
I might like to get into it more—
netball I mean. Maybe I could play
in a team or something, like you do."

Rachel "Great idea! You should come to training with me sometime."

Ellie "How could I? Aren't you forgetting that I'm hopeless at most sports?"

Rachel "Oh yes. I remember when you had a go at tennis. You threw your racquet into the air and nearly knocked out some pigeons!"

Both girls giggle.

Rachel has another shot at the ring and shoots another goal.

Rachel "Maybe you just haven't found a sport that suits you. I wouldn't give up yet. Netball just might end up being your thing."

Ellie "Do you think?"

Rachel "You never know till you give it a go. Here, have a shot."

Rachel hands the ball to Ellie.

Rachel "Come on. You can do it. Ready? Shoot!"

CHAPTER 2

Ball Robbers

Ellie aims, then throws the netball
up towards the ring. It's such an
awful shot that the ball whizzes past
the ring and over the fence that
surrounds the court.

Ellie "See, I'm terrible."

Rachel "No, you're not. It's only your first shot. You just didn't realise how strong you are."

While the girls talk, the ball is gaining speed as it rolls down the hill.

Rachel "Hey, the ball!"

Ellie "Hurry, before it hits the football pitch and those two boys!"

The two girls chase after the ball. It lands on the football pitch at the bottom of the hill.

Ellie "Hey! What are those boys doing? They're stealing my netball."

Rachel "They better not be!"

Rachel sprints towards the boys.
Ellie, who is feeling a bit nervous,
waits for a moment then follows.
By the time Ellie catches up with
Rachel the boys have raced off with
the ball in the direction of the
netball court.

Ellie "What did you say to them? How come they still have my ball?"

Rachel "I said I'd challenge them to a netball shoot-out to get the ball back. And they laughed but said OK. Now, there's a catch ..."

Ellie "I don't like the sound of this."

Rachel "We all have to take two shots each. The team with the most goals wins the ball. It's going to be a netball showdown!"

Ellie "You're not meaning me too, are you? Why me? I'm terrible. That's why we're in this mess. You can take my shots for me."

Rachel "But we both have to shoot—
it's that or nothing. We can beat
these wimpy boys. Boys can't play
netball anyway."

Ellie "I hope you're right."

The girls head back to the netball
court where the two boys are waiting
with Ellie's ball.

CHAPTER 3

Bulldog Boy and Snail Boy

The boys choose Ellie to go first in the netball showdown. Ellie throws her two shots. As predicted, she misses both times.

Ellie "Sorry Rachel."

Rachel "Don't worry yet. Let me sink my two in and hopefully they'll miss their shots."

As Rachel prepares to take her first shot at goal, the boys try to put her off by putting their fingers inside their mouths and making popping noises.

Rachel "If you boys don't pack it in, I'm going to ..."

Ellie "Ignore them, Rachel. Don't get them mad. Look how big they are."

Rachel (whispering) "They look like two big baboons. Actually, the smaller one looks like a bulldog with his little pug nose and droopy eyes. He's Bulldog Boy!"

Ellie "Yes, and did you see how slowly the other one runs?"

Ellie and Rachel "Well, he can be Snail Boy from now on!"

Rachel takes her shot and the ball swishes through the ring.

Ellie (excitedly) "Yes! How's that, Snail Boy and ... oops! I mean ..."

The boys sneer at the girls.

Rachel "She said 'make it sail, boy'. She sometimes calls me 'boy'."

Rachel takes her second shot. Again, she gets it in.

Rachel "Yes! That's two for the girls. Now it's your turn, losers."

Rachel winks at Ellie as she tosses the ball to the boys. Snail Boy takes his shots. He misses the first but gets his second throw in. Then it's Bulldog Boy's first turn. He also gets a goal.

Rachel "It's two goals all. If he gets this one ..."

Ellie "If he gets this one, it's goodbye to my new ball forever! Miss, miss, please miss."

Bulldog Boy throws the netball high into the air. It floats for several seconds before dropping directly through the middle of the ring. The boys win.

Ellie "I don't believe it! Mum's going
to kill me! We've got to get my ball
back."

Rachel "Don't worry, I've got
another idea."

CHAPTER 4

It's Not Over Yet

The boys race off with Ellie's new
netball. Rachel catches up with them
and says something to Snail Boy.
Ellie watches. A minute later, Rachel
returns.

Ellie "What did you say to them?
    Will I get my netball back?"
Rachel "Well, sort of."
Ellie "Sort of? What do you mean
    sort of?"

Rachel "Well, I tried to get them to have another netball showdown."

Ellie "What?"

Rachel "But they said no."

Ellie "Good. I couldn't take losing again."

Rachel "So I challenged them to a football penalty shoot-out instead."

Emma "You did what?"

Rachel "It's the only way we've got any hope of getting your ball back."

Ellie "No, it isn't. I'm going to tell my dad what's happened."

Rachel "OK. But by the time you do that they'll be long gone, laughing their heads off. And they'll get home and *still* be making fun of us. Imagine if they took the ball to some secret hideaway on a deserted island and gave it magical powers and …"

Ellie "Dream on!"

Rachel "Mmm. Maybe not, but let's do this football thing and show them. I said we'd meet at the football pitch. We all have to take a penalty shot for goal, the team with the most goals will win your ball."

Ellie "From netball to football. This is just crazy. But let's go and get it over with."

CHAPTER 5

Final Showdown

Ellie and Rachel meet the boys in front of the football goal. The boys decide to kick for goals first so Rachel is goalie. Snail Boy lines up his penalty shot and kicks the ball hard. Rachel dives to her left and punches the ball away.

Ellie (shouting) "I don't believe it! That was amazing. You saved it."

Rachel "I know. How good was that!"

As Snail Boy stamps his foot in frustration, Bulldog Boy prepares to take his shot. He takes a long run up and … *thump!* The ball whizzes over Rachel and the crossbar, missing the goal completely.

Rachel "Yes! No score to the boys. This is our chance, Ellie. I'll go first. I know I can get a goal. Then we can grab your ball and we're out of here!"

Rachel places the netball on the penalty spot with Snail Boy as goalie. Rachel takes in a deep breath and ... *thump!* She kicks the ball hard along the ground but Snail Boy stops it with his foot and saves it.

Ellie "Oh no, my turn. We'll lose again, for sure!"

Rachel "Sorry Ellie, but if you miss, we're history. So go on, take your shot."

Ellie (sighing) "OK, here goes nothing."

Ellie places the ball on the penalty spot and takes a few steps back. She runs at the ball and boots it as hard as she can. The ball flies through the air at an incredible speed. It zips past Snail Boy and into the back of the net. It's a goal!

Rachel "Woo hoo! You got it! You got it!"

Ellie "I know, I know! I got it! I got it!"

The boys toss the netball back at the girls and storm off in a huff.

Rachel "Ellie, you got your ball back.
And you know what this means?"

Ellie "What?"

Rachel "Football's your sport. Forget
netball, you're a football star!"

Ellie "Wow, I guess I am."

free pass You get a free pass when the player you're playing against does something wrong.

offside When a player crosses into an area that they are not allowed to be in.

three seconds A penalty against a player who holds the ball for more than three seconds before passing it.

throw in One team gets to throw the ball in from the sideline if the other team makes the ball go out of the court.

toss-up When both players have possession of the ball, it is tossed into the air between them. The one that catches it first gets to pass.

GIRLS ROCK!
Netball Must-dos

☆ You must pass the ball or shoot for a goal within three seconds.

☆ Practise shouting out loudly, to get your team mates attention.

☆ Remember to take off all your jewellery before playing so you won't poke or scratch anyone, including yourself!

☆ Cheer for your team mates, and encourage them if they do something good.

☆ Practise whenever and wherever you can. Try throwing a netball into a bucket in your garden.

☆ Shake your opponent's hand after the game, even if your team loses.

☆ Bring something warm to wear after the game. Remember, netball's a winter sport!

☆ Make up a team chant to perform with your team members before your game—it will really put you in the mood!

GIRLS ROCK!

Netball Instant Info

 Australia has won more world netball championships than any other country.

 The longest match of netball ever played lasted 50 hours. That game was played in South Africa in 2001.

 A netball court is 30.5 metres long and 15.25 metres wide.

 A netball court is divided into three sections.

 Netballs are usually made from leather or rubber.

A netball weighs between 400 and 500 grams.

 Each player wears a bib with the initials for their position e.g. "GA" is "Goal Attack". These make the positions clear to the players, spectators and umpires.

 The first world netball championships were held in England in 1963.

 Netball is not an Olympic sport but hopefully it will be in the future.

GIRLS ROCK!

Think Tank

1 How can you practise shooting goals at home if you don't have a netball ring?

2 What should you do if boys steal your netball?

3 What animals do the boys in the story remind the girls of?

4 What is a "free pass" (not the kind your Grandma uses on the bus)?

5 How high do you think the netball hoop is—2.4 metres or 1 metre?

6 What is one of the best ways to make sure your netball team wins?

7 Who wears a bib in netball?

8 Which season is netball played in?

Answers

8 Netball is played in winter.

7 All players wear a bib to show what position they are playing.

6 Make up a team chant and recite it before each game—your team is sure to win!

5 A netball hoop is 2.4 metres high.

4 A free pass is given to the other player when you do something wrong.

3 The boys remind the girls of a bulldog and a snail.

2 You challenge them to a football shoot-out.

1 You can practise shooting at home by throwing the ball into a bucket.

How did you score?

- If you got 8 answers correct, then maybe you should try out for the England netball team.

- If you got 6 or more answers correct, you like netball and probably already play in a team. If you don't, maybe you should try it.

- If you got fewer than 4 answers correct, then maybe you might like to try football.

Hey Girls!

I hope that you have as much fun reading my story as I have had writing it. I loved reading and writing stories when I was young.

Here are some suggestions that might help you enjoy reading even more than you do now.

At school, why don't you use "Netball Showdown" as a play? You and your friends can be the actors. Get some netball bibs (make your own if you can't get hold of any) and a ball to use as props. So ... have you decided who is going to be Ellie and who is going to be Rachel? And what about the narrator?

Now act out the story in front of your friends. I'm sure you'll all have a great time!

You also might like to take this story home and get someone in your family to read it with you. Maybe they can take on a part in the story.

Whatever you choose to do, you can have as much fun with reading and writing as a polar bear has in a freezer!

And remember, Girls Rock!

Jacqueline Srena

GIRLS ROCK!

When We Were Kids

Jacqueline · Shey

Jacqueline talked to Shey, another
Girls Rock! author.

Jacqueline "Were you good at netball when you were young?"

Shey "Yes, still am. I'm a champion!"

Jacqueline "Really?"

Shey "Yes, I'm so good that I played for England."

Jacqueline "That's unreal!"

Shey "I was really disappointed, though. We won, but I never got my medal!"

Jacqueline "Why not?"

Shey "Mum woke me up just before they presented me with mine!"

GIRLS ROCK!
What A Laugh!

Q How do netballers stay cool during a game?

A They stand near a netball fan!

GIRLS ROCK!

Read about the fun
that girls have in these
GIRLS ROCK! titles:

The Sleepover

Pool Pals

Bowling Buddies

Girl Pirates

Netball Showdown

School Play Stars

Diary Disaster

Horsing Around

GIRLS ROCK! books are available from
most booksellers. For mail order information
please call Rising Stars on 0870 40 20 40 8 or visit
www.risingstars-uk.com